KU-468-020

To everyone who read the last three

Bunny vs Monkey: Book Four
is A DAVID FICKLING BOOK

First published in Great Britain in 2017 by
David Fickling Books,
31 Beaumont Street,
Oxford, OX1 2NP

Text and illustrations © Jamie Smart, 2017

978-1-910989-79-1

All rights reserved.

1 3 5 7 9 10 8 6 4 2

The right of Jamie Smart to be identified as the author and illustrator of this work has
been asserted by him in accordance with the Copyright, Designs and Patents Act 1988.

All rights reserved. No part of this publication may be reproduced,
stored in a retrieval system, or transmitted in any form or by any means,
electronic, mechanical, photocopying, recording or otherwise,
without the prior permission of the publishers.

David Fickling Books reg. no. 8340307

A CIP catalogue record for this book
is available from the British Library.

Printed and bound in Great Britain by Sterling.

Papers used by David Fickling Books are from
well-managed forests and other responsible sources.

CONTENTS

JULY

PAGE 6 – "A NEW CHALLENGER APPEARS"
PAGE 8 – "SEE-SAW!"
PAGE 10 – "GRAV-O-BOX"
PAGE 12 – "AROUND THE WOODS IN 80 SECONDS"

AUGUST

PAGE 14 – "FAT MONKEY"
PAGE 16 – "MONKEY AT WORK"
PAGE 18 – "THE WOBBLES!"
PAGE 20 – "BATTLE STATIONS"
PAGE 22 – "THE VINES"

SEPTEMBER

PAGE 24 – "POINK"
PAGE 26 – "MONKEYTRON!"
PAGE 28 – "A PIG ON THE RANGE"
PAGE 30 – "A BEAR BUM!"

OCTOBER

PAGE 32 – "THE INCREDIBLE METAL STEVE"
PAGE 34 – "BUNNY VS MONKEY!"
PAGE 36 – "CATCH THAT BUNNY"
PAGE 38 – "WORMS"

NOVEMBER

PAGE 40 – "GOODBYE, BUNNY"
PAGE 42 – "ARISE, LORD WUFFYWUFF!"
PAGE 44 – "THE THING!"
PAGE 46 – "A PLACE WHERE YOU BELONG"
PAGE 48 – "ONCE UPON A TIME"

DECEMBER

PAGE 52 – "CHOOSE YOUR SIDE!"
PAGE 54 – "SNOW MEANIES"
PAGE 56 – "THE REAL SANTA!"
PAGE 60 – "DOOR B"

"SEE-SAW!"

WHAT IS THIS PLACE?

THIS IS **MY** ADVENTURE PLAYGROUND. I FOUND IT, SO IT IS **MINE**.

NO BUNNIES ALLOWED!

IT'S A BIT RUBBISH, THOUGH. EVERYTHING'S BROKEN.

WHAT HAPPENED HERE?

FIVE MINUTES EARLIER...

HAMMER HAMMER HAMMER HAMMER HAMMER HAMMER

SMASH!

I DUNNO. IT'S A MYSTERY. WHAT ARE **YOU** DOING HERE?

I'VE BEEN OUT CLEANING UP DEER POO!

DEER POO

I DO WISH THEY'D PICK IT UP THEMSELVES.

WELL, YOU CAN GO NOW. YOU ARE NOT WORTHY TO COME AND PLAY IN **MY** TERRIBLE PLAYGROUND.

THERE MUST BE SOMETHING STILL IN ONE PIECE.

A SEE-SAW!

NOW **THAT** WAS BROKEN WHEN I GOT HERE.

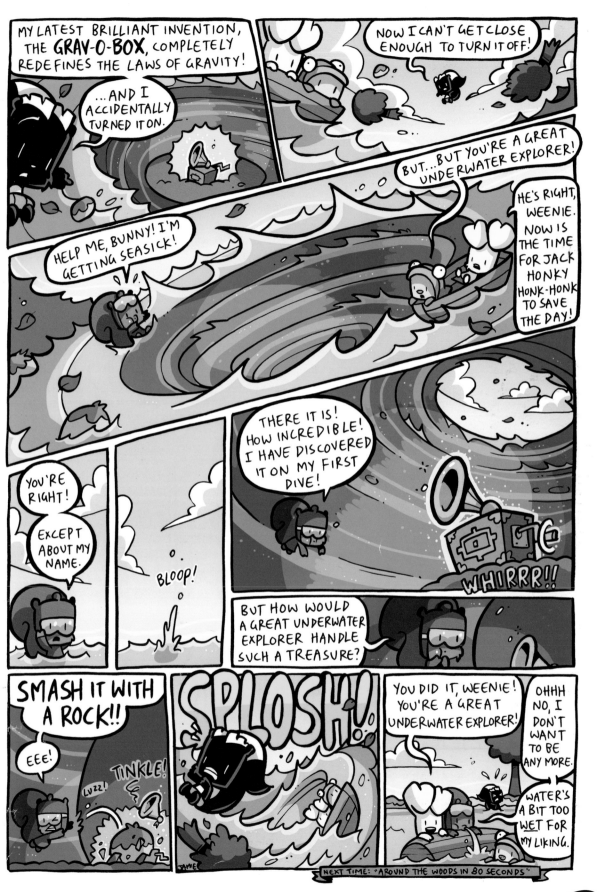

PUFF! PUFF!

GLUB GLUB!

DOOF DOOF!

A LITTLE WHILE LATER...

I DID IT! I HAVE RETURNED TO MY ORIGINAL TONED PHYSIQUE!

I AM A MONKEY ADONIS!

GOOD. NOW GIVE WEENIE HIS CAKES BACK.

HA HA HA HA.

NOPE.

IF I AM EVER GOING TO BE **GLORIOUS MONKEY EMPEROR**, THEN I MUST ALWAYS BE AS CRUEL AS POSSIBLE!

CHOMP! CHOMP!

HAR HAR NOM!

FWRRRRP!

!!

AARGH, I GOT ALL FAT AGAIN! CURSE MY MONKEY METABOLISM!

YOU JUST UNDID ALL YOUR HARD WORK BY BEING SPITEFUL.

GOOD.

AM I GOING TO STARVE THIS WINTER, BUNNY?

HANG ON WEENIE, YOU DON'T EVEN HIBERNATE.

OH.

OH YEAH.

BOO HOO HOO

YAY YYY YYY!

EPILOGUE!

GENTLEMEN, DO YOU REMEMBER WHEN WE HERE AT THE BRITISH SPACE PROGRAMME FIRED A **MONKEY** INTO SPACE?

VAAAGUELY.

WELL, WE PICKED UP A CURIOUS TRACKING SIGNAL.

AND WE FOUND HIM. RIGHT HERE ON EARTH.

GOOD GRIEF, CAN'T HAVE BEEN HARD TO SPOT HIM.

IS HE...IS HE CRYING?

IT DOESN'T MATTER.

THAT IS OUR MONKEY...

...AND WE MUST GET HIM BACK.

NEXT TIME: "MONKEY AT WORK"

15

SEE? A BRILLIANT STASH OF MACHINERY, TOOLS, AND **MORE MACHINERY!**

OH NO! THIS IS TERRIBLE.

WORK STATION OUTPOST

MACHINERY, BUNNY. **CAN YOU IMAGINE MY FACE?!!**

SO!

HAPPY!

THE HUMANS MUST BE CLOSER THAN WE THOUGHT. REMEMBER THE HUMANS, MONKEY? THEY WANT TO BUILD A ROAD THROUGH OUR WOODS.

I KNOW! I'VE SEEN THEIR PLANS!

IT LOOKS BUHH-RILLIANT.

EEK, THEY'RE COMING BACK!

HIDE!

WHEE!

SCARPER!

I STILL DON'T GET IT, CLAUDE. ONE OF OUR DIGGERS IS DEFINITELY MISSING.

THAT WAS **ME!**

MMF!

MONKEY, WE HAVE TO MAKE THEM **LEAVE!**

NO! THEY ARE MY **FRIENDS.**

FINE. IF YOU WON'T HELP, THEN IT'S UP TO THE REST OF US. I'M TIRED OF RUNNING AND HIDING WHENEVER HUMANS COME INTO OUR WOODS.

IT'S ABOUT TIME WE MADE A STAND, TO USE THE RESOURCES OF NATURE.

...TO DEFEND OUR WOODS!

SPLOSH!

WORK STATION OUTPOST

WHEEE! I'M A **WATER-PIG!**

OR, WE COULD DO THAT.

RRGH! THWARTED BY MY OWN PIPEWORK!

SPLISH! SPLISH!

NEXT TIME: "THE WOBBLES!"

17

"THE WOBBLES!"

WHAT ON EARTH IS IT?

CAN I HUUUG IT?

IT SMELLS LIKE GRAVY!

I REALISED THERE WEREN'T ENOUGH ANIMALS IN THE WORLD, SO I DECIDED TO CREATE MY OWN!

I CALL IT THE WOBBLE.

IT LIVES ON A DIET OF CUSTARD, AND DOES LITTLE MORE THAN 'MEEP'.

MEEP!

BUT IT IS MINE. I MADE IT.

CUSTARD-O-M

W...WHY IS IT SHAKING?

GOODNESS, I'M NOT SURE. TO BRING IT TO LIFE, I DID HAVE TO SET ITS PARTICLES TO A VERY HIGH VIBRATION.

MEEP! MEEP! MEEP! MEEP!

BANG!

SHRIEK!

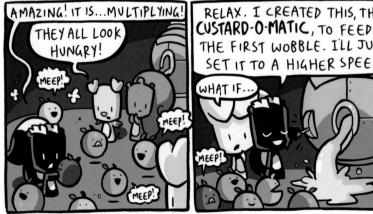

AMAZING! IT IS...MULTIPLYING!

THEY ALL LOOK HUNGRY!

MEEP!

MEEP!

MEEP!

RELAX. I CREATED THIS, THE CUSTARD-O-MATIC, TO FEED THE FIRST WOBBLE. I'LL JUST SET IT TO A HIGHER SPEED!

WHAT IF...

MEEP!

WHAT IF THE WOBBLES KEEP MULTIPLYING?

THEN, UM... THEN...

BANG!

BAN

"BATTLE STATIONS"

THE HUMANS ARE COMING!

THE HUMANS ARE COMING!

WE WERE PUTTING CUSTARD ON PIG'S HEAD, WHEN WE SAW ONE! HEADING THIS WAY!

SO, THEY'RE FINALLY INVADING.

WELL, WE ARE READY!

OPERATION **DEFEND THE WOODS** IS GO!

EVERYONE! TO YOUR DEFENCES!

PIG? WEENIE? WHY ARE YOU HIDING?

WE'RE GOING TO THROW **PLASTIC SPOONS** AT THEM!

THAT'S NOT REALLY... AUGH!

CREEEEAK!

DID I RELEASE IT TOO SOON?

BE CAREFUL, MONKEY. <u>MY</u> DEFENCE IS A **CHICKEN CANNON!**

IT IS A VERY SENSITIVE DEVICE. ONE WRONG MOVE, AND...

...I'VE PRESSED THE WRONG BUTTON! **EVERYONE RUN!**

FRRPP!!

RUN!

CLUCK!!

WHAT ABOUT METAL STEVE? SURELY **HE** CAN HELP US?

OH, UMM... I FORGOT TO CHARGE HIM UP THIS MORNING.

SORRY.

THIS IS OUR BIG CHANCE TO DEFEND OURSELVES, AND IT'S ALL GONE **WRONG!**

IDIOTS.

I HAD THE BEST IDEA.

WE CAN **HIDE**, IN THE IMPENETRABLE **PANIC ROOM**, WHICH I BUILT BESIDE BUNNY'S HOUSE.

WHAT?

HOW COME I NEVER KNEW THIS WAS HERE?

YOU FORGET THINGS.

INSIDE, QUICKLY.

WE LOCK IT, AND NOW...

NOW WE SHH.

AHH! THE PEACE AND TRANQUILLITY OF NATURE!

SLAM!

THAT'S STRANGE. WHO WOULD BUILD A LITTLE HOUSE ALL THE WAY OUT HERE IN THE WOODS?

FART!

HEE HEE! =MMF!=

SHH!

SHH-HH!

HUH.

AH WELL.

I THINK WE'RE SAFE. WHAT DO WE DO NOW, LE FOX?

WE WAIT...

WE WAIT A LONG TIME.

...OR UNTIL I REMEMBER HOW WE GET OUT OF HERE!

ARGH!

NEXT TIME: "THE VINES"

"THE VINES"

TUM TE TUM TE TUM!

WEENIE? HOW LONG HAVE YOU LIVED IN A WOODLAND VILLAGE HIGH UP IN THE TREES?

I COME UP HERE TO GET AWAY FROM THINGS, BUNNY. THIS IS THE VILLAGE MY SQUIRREL ANCESTORS BUILT LONG AGO.

THEY CALLED IT... SQUIRRELVILLE!

BUNNY, HOW LONG HAVE YOU BEEN FLOATING UP AS HIGH AS SQUIRRELVILLE?

OH, UM...

AUGH! I WASN'T PAYING ATTENTION, CLEARLY. AUGH!

UH, BUNNY? YOU MIGHT WANT TO GET DOWN.

YOU'RE TELLING ME!

NO, SERIOUSLY. THE VINES ARE FAR MORE...

...UNSTABLE

...THAN I HAD PLANNED.

CRASH!

SQUIRRELVILLE!

AND HERRE WE GO...

SHRIEK!

SIGH

'POINK!'

SHRIIIIII-IIIIIEK!

WHAT FOUL TERROR TORMENTS POOR PIG?

WHAT MALEFICENT FATE?

WHAT THE HECK IS GOING ON?!

DON'T LET IT GET ME, BUNNY! I'M TOO PRETTY!

WHAT? WHAT'S GOING TO GET YOU?

OH.

WHERE'D HE GO?

POINK! SHRIEK!

HA HAAA!

YOU'VE BEEN **POINKED**, BUNNY! NOW YOU ARE THE **POINKER**! AND UNLESS YOU CAN **POINK** SOMEONE ELSE...

...YOU'LL BE **FOREVER POINKED!**

SHRIIIIIIIEK!

I'M NOT PLAYING THIS...

...STUPID...

UM...

WAIT FOR ME!

GET AWAY, POINKER!

"MONKEY -TRON!"

SKUNKY, I'M STILL A LAUGHING STOCK IN THE WOODS. **NO ONE** FEARS ME!

I NEED YOUR HELP, BUT I'VE TRIED ALL YOUR INVENTIONS ALREADY.

WELL, NOT QUITE ALL.

SQUID-U-LIKE

THERE IS ONE THING I'VE BEEN HOLDING BACK.

JUST UNTIL YOU'RE READY TO USE IT.

SECRET!

THIS INVENTION WILL BE WHAT GRANTS YOU ULTIMATE POWER OVER THE REST OF US. IT IS TAILOR-MADE TO YOU, AND YOU ALONE. BUT I'M ONLY TELLING YOU ABOUT IT TO SHOW OFF. THIS LEVEL OF AWESOME IS TOO DANGEROUS!

YOU CAN'T HAVE IT YET.

AW C'MON, I'LL GIVE YOU THIS CHEESE.

CHEESE! GO ON, THEN.

MEANWHILE, ABOVE GROUND...

IT IS IMPERATIVE WE TRAP THAT MONKEY, AND BRING HIM BACK TO THE LAB.

TRAP!

MEH HEH!

WHAT'S WRONG WITH HIM?

OH, TERRY'S JUST HAD TOO MUCH SUGAR.

BZZZ! S

HE'S JUST HERE TO CARRY THE EQUIPMENT.

CRUNCH!

SHHH!

CRUNCH!

IS IT... THE MONKEY?

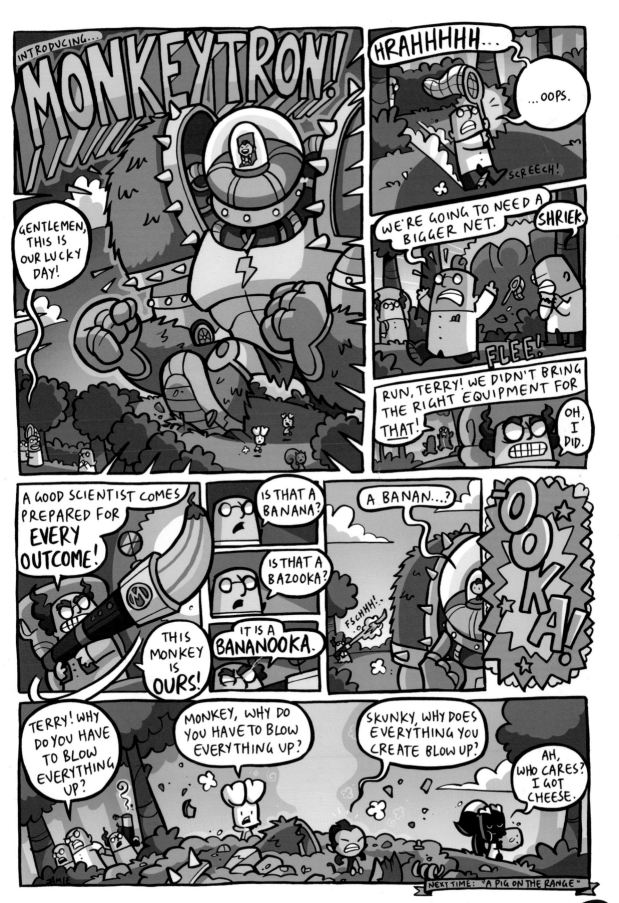

GOOD MORNING, COUSIN GABE!

≡SNORT!≡
PIG?

MMF.

WELL HOWDY DOODY, COUSIN PIG! ABOUT TIME YOU CAME BACK, I'VE JUST BEEN RUSTLING UP SOME DELICIOUS TURNIPS FOR LUNCH!

WHAT IS IT YOU DO IN THOSE WOODS, ANYWAY?

UM. NOT MUCH.

PIG! SO NICE TO SEE OUR WANDERING SON AGAIN.

PIGGY WIGGY! YEEEE!

AND YOU'RE JUST IN TIME FOR A DELIGHTFUL SWILL LUNCH!

BUT... MY TURNIPS!

DON'T BE SILLY, GABE. THE HUMANS GIVE US ALL WE NEED!

SPTHBTHLOP!

SO... CHOMP... TELL US, YOUNG PIG. WHAT SIGHTS HAVE YOU SEEN? WHAT AMAZING ADVENTURES HAVE YOU HAD?

UM... CHOMP... NOTHING?

CHOMP!
CHOMP!
CHOMP!
CHOMP!

NONSENSE! YOU'RE THE WISEST AND BRAVEST OF ALL US PIGS. OF COURSE YOU HAVE STORIES TO TELL!

WELL, UM, THIS ONE TIME I DID A FART UNDERWATER.

AND IT ALL BUBBLED UP! HEE HEE HEE THPTHBTHH!

HEE HEE!

HEE!

SNORT!

CHOMP CHOMP CHOMP

AND SO, OFF PIG GOES AGAIN, LEAVING ONE FAMILY...

...FOR ANOTHER.

PIG! WHERE HAVE YOU BEEN?

UM, I CAN'T REMEMBER.

WELL, GET TOOLED UP! WE'RE DEFENDING OURSELVES AGAINST THE TERRIBLE HUMANS!

(HOWEVER CRAZY THEY MIGHT BE)

NEXT TIME: "A BEAR BUM!"

29

"A BEAR BUM!"

I HAVE HAD IT WITH THESE WOODS. STRANGE NOISES, WEIRD EXPLOSIONS, SOMETHING IS GOING ON!

AND IF THE NATIONAL WOODLAND ASSOCIATION WON'T INVESTIGATE...

...THEN IT IS UP TO ME, PARK RANGER DEREK P. BRIGSTOCKE, TO UNCOVER THE TRUTH!

I JUST HOPE THE TRUTH IS NOTHING SCARY...

...OOPF!

GRRRWLL!

A...GRIZZLY BEAR IN...

A...

...NET?

SCREEEEEEEEEAM!!

GRRRRRWLLLLLLL!!

HMM.

THIS IS GOING TO BE A PROBLEM.

THAT NET WAS MEANT TO CATCH HUMANS, TO HELP US DEFEND THE WOODS. I WASN'T EXPECTING THE BEAR TO GET CAUGHT IN IT!

HEE HEE. SILLY BEAR.

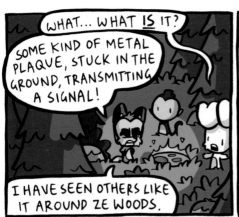

WHAT... WHAT **IS** IT?

SOME KIND OF METAL PLAQUE, STUCK IN THE GROUND, TRANSMITTING A SIGNAL!

I HAVE SEEN OTHERS LIKE IT AROUND ZE WOODS.

YEAH WELL, IF THIS THING BROUGHT STEVE DOWN...

MAYBE IT CAN CHARGE HIM BACK UP!

. . . .

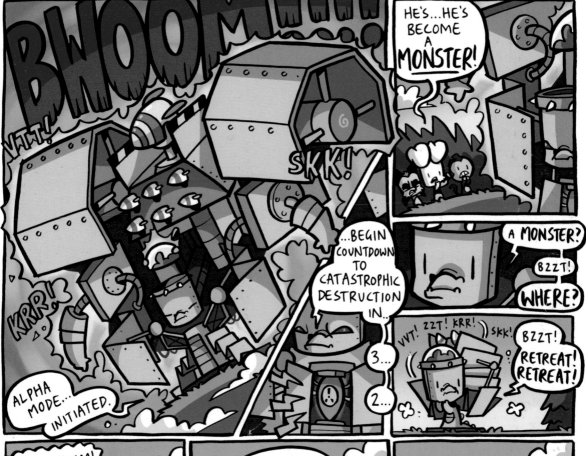

BWOOM!!!!!

VVT!

SKK!

KRR!

BEGIN COUNTDOWN TO CATASTROPHIC DESTRUCTION IN...

3...

2...

ALPHA MODE... INITIATED.

HE'S...HE'S BECOME A **MONSTER!**

A MONSTER?

BZZT!

WHERE?

VVT! ZZT! KRR! SKK!

BZZT! RETREAT! RETREAT!

SCREEEAMM!

BZZT! WAIT FOR ME!

WILL YOU LOT STOP JUMPING AROUND ON MY **ROOF?!**

NEXT TIME: "BUNNY VS MONKEY!"

33

"BUNNY -VS- MONKEY!"

MONKEY WHAT HAVE YOU **DONE**?

I'VE DESTROYED YOUR HOUSE!

I'VE DONE IT ENOUGH TIMES, IT'S WEIRD YOU DON'T KNOW BY NOW.

RRRGHH! THIS IS THE **LAST STRAW,** YOU HORRIBLE CREATURE!

HAR HAR, WHAT'RE YOU GOING TO DO? YOU'RE JUST A BUNNY, WHEREAS I AM A **GREAT AND POWERFUL MONKEY!**

BLAT!!

EUGH.

DID YOU JUST THROW MY SANDWICH?

COME AT ME, MONKEY! LET'S SORT THIS OUT ONCE AND FOR ALL!

GAH! IF HE'S ALLOWED TO USE WEAPONS, THEN SO AM I! SKUNKY, WHAT WEAPONS DO YOU HAVE ON YOU?

UMM...

ONLY THIS **HIGHLY VOLATILE TICKING BOMB!** BUT IF IT BLEW UP, YOU'D BE CAUGHT IN THE BLAST TOO!

TICK!

TICK!

00:00

A BOMB? HA! WHAT ARE YOU GOING TO DO, HIT ME WITH IT?

TICK! TICK!

CLONK!

YES.

OW!

SERIOUSLY, MONKEY. YOU SHOULDN'T... OW!!

QUIET, SCIENCE!

CLONK!

NO-ONE WILL DEFEAT ME! I AM EMPEROR MONK... OOF!!

MY PUDDING!

LUZZ!

HRR-RAR-RGHHLE!

BLARR-RGLEF!

CLONK!
SPLAT!
CLONK!
OOF!
CLONK!
FRRP!
CLONK!
ARGH!

SOME TIME LATER...

PHEW! I'M EXHAUSTED! WE CAN'T KEEP FIGHTING FOREVER.

AGREED.

A TRUCE, THEN. AN ARMISTICE. WE AGREE TO RESPECT EACH OTHER'S BOUNDARIES.

CLONK!

NO. LET ME WIN.

BOOM!

I DID WARN HIM.

YOU'RE SO STUPID, MONKEY! WHY CAN'T YOU DO ANYTHING RIGHT?

YOU SHUTTING UP WOULD BE NICE. I'LL DO THAT.

CLONK!

SIGHH..

JAMIE

NEXT TIME: "CATCH THAT BUNNY!"

35

HE'S RUNNING!

SO MUCH FOR STEALTH, THEN!

GRAB HIM!!

HE'LL BE DELICIOUS!

RUN, BUNNY!

HAR HAR! YOU FELL RIGHT INTO OUR TRAP!

WHAT?

HOP!

WE GOT HIM CORNERED!

THERE HE IS!

LOOK INTO THE EYES OF THE **HYPNO-MONKEY**, FOOLISH MORTALS! SLIP INTO MY HYPNOTIC GAAAAAZE.

MESMERISE!

NOW, TELL US EVERYTHING YOU KNOW ABOUT THE ROAD BEING BUILT. GIVE US ALL YOUR HUMAN KNOWLEDGE!

BUHHHHHH...

OH, AND ONE MORE THING...

I DON'T LIKE WORKING WITH YOU, SKUNKY, ESPECIALLY NOT AS B**A**IT.

YOU WERE RUBBISH BAIT. THEY KNEW NOTHING.

WILL THEY BE OKAY?

OH, THEY'LL BE FINE.

TOMORROW.

DOODLE DOOO!

CLUCK! CLUCK!

BUCK-**CAW!** CLUCK CLUCK!

PECK! PECK!

JAMIE

NEXT TIME: "WORMS"

37

"WORMS"

EARLY MORNING, AND THE AIR IS FILLED WITH THE MELODIC CALLS OF THE WOODLAND ANIMALS...

YAH YAH YAH YAH!

FRPP!

BOO BOO BOO BOO THPTHBH!

STOMP! STOMP!

BAM! BAM!

STOMP! STOMP!

BUT WHAT FIERCE CREATURE IS THIS, SPEEDING TOWARDS THEM?

RUMMMMBLE!

DO YOU KNOW WHAT TIME IT IS? WHAT IS WRONG WITH YOU TWO?

AH, IT'S AN ANGRY BUNNY.

DID WE WAKE YOU, BUNNY?

SOMEHOW, YES.

WE'RE TRYING TO WAKE UP THE WORMS! WHILE IT'S RAINING AND EARLY IN THE MORNING IS THE BEST TIME!

THE...WHAT?

THE WORMS! IF YOU MAKE A LOT OF NOISE, THEY COME OUT OF THE GROUND!

STOMP! STOMP!

I'VE NEVER HEARD ANYTHING SO RIDICU....

POP!

EEE!!

IT WORKED! IT WORKED!

POP!
POP!
POP!
POP!

THEY'VE ALL COME UP TO SEE WHAT'S GOING ON!

WHAT EXACTLY ARE YOU GOING TO DO WITH ALL THESE WORMS?

A WORM HAT!

A WORM PIE!

UGH!

ONLY JOKING. WE'RE GOING TO TAKE THEM DOWN TO THE RIVER AND DO SOME FISHING!

FISHING? THEY'RE BAIT? AFTER ALL THAT, YOU'RE GOING TO LET THE WORMS GET EATEN BY FISH?

CLONK!
CLONK!

NO, SILLY. EUGH! WE BROUGHT THE WORMS DOWN TO WATCH US FISH!

WE THOUGHT THEY MIGHT ENJOY IT.

BUT THEN, HOW ARE YOU GOING TO GET THE FISH OUT OF THE WATER?

WELL, DUHHH...

YAH YAH YAH YAH!

FRPP!

!BANG!
BANG!
BANG!

BOO BOO BOO BOO THPTBTH!

HOW SILLY OF ME.

JAMIE

NEXT TIME: "GOODBYE, BUNNY."

39

NOVEMBER

"GOODBYE, BUNNY"

ONE COLD WINTER'S MORNING, BUNNY WAS STANDING INSIDE HIS HOUSE, STARING OUT OF THE WINDOW...

HE WAS LOOKING AT THE WOODS HE LOVED SO MUCH...

CARROTS

RROTS

THE ONLY WOODS HE KNEW...

CAR

HE WATCHED HIS WOODLAND FRIENDS PLAYING ON THE GRASS...

I AM SIR CHUFFINGTON, THE KNIGHT!

AND I AM LORD WUFFYWUFF, THE LUNCHTIME!

HAVE AT YE!

CRUMP!!

OWWW!

BOO HOO HOO!

BOO HOO!

AND JUST THEN, SOMETHING OCCURRED TO BUNNY THAT HE'D NEVER BEEN ABLE TO PUT INTO WORDS BEFORE...

I DON'T BELONG HERE.

NO, YOU DON'T.

SHRIEK! LE FOX! HOW DID YOU GET IN?

I DUG A TUNNEL UNDER YOUR FLOOR. SO WHAT? CARRY ON.

I'VE FELT THIS WAY FOR A WHILE, LE FOX. I CAN'T EXPLAIN IT, I JUST KNOW THIS ISN'T MY HOME.

WHERE **IS** YOUR HOME THEN?

I DON'T KNOW. BUT FOR AS LONG AS I CAN REMEMBER, I'VE HAD THIS BOX.

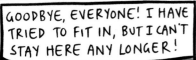

AND INSIDE THIS BOX LIES THE ANSWER!

I HAVE TO GO. I'LL PACK A FEW THINGS, AND GO OUT INTO THE WORLD.

TO DISCOVER WHERE I CAME FROM, AND FIND OUT WHO I AM.

ISN'T THAT THE MOST IMPORTANT THING?

WHY DO I HAVE SO MANY CARROTS?

I DON'T EVEN LIKE CARROTS!

GOODBYE, EVERYONE! I HAVE TRIED TO FIT IN, BUT I CAN'T STAY HERE ANY LONGER!

BUNNY, NO! WE MADE YOU A CAKE!

WELL, WE MADE A CAKE. LAST WEEK.

THERE ARE STILL SOME CRUMBS OF IT IN MY BELLY, IF YOU WANT THEM.

BUNNY? GOING? AT LAST, I CAN TAKE OVER THE WOODS!

YOU WON'T, MONKEY. IT'LL GO WRONG, LIKE ALWAYS.

BAH! I SUPPOSE!

HE'S LEAVING?

WHAT DID HE FIND OUT?

CLANK! CLANK!

NOTHING. BUT THERE IS A BOX.

WHAT'S IN THE BOX?

PLEASE CONTACT: 15 BRAMBLE CRESCENT MIDDLETON, THE CITY

YOU WILL ALL BE FINE WITHOUT ME.

YOU MUST HAVE BEEN BEFORE.

BUT...BUT WHO'LL HELP ME CLIMB BACK OUT WHEN I FALL IN A HOLE?

I THINK YOU'RE GOING TO HAVE TO START DOING THAT FOR YOURSELF, PIG.

JAMIE

BUNNY WILL RETURN...

...HOPEFULLY!

"A PLACE WHERE YOU BELONG"

SOMEWHERE IN THE CITY...

LUNCHTIME!

TODAY IT'S **CARRO**— OH, YOU STILL HAVEN'T EATEN YOUR BREAKFAST.

BUNNY

SIGH...

OR ANY OF YOUR MEALS FROM THE LAST FEW WEEKS.

YOU ALWAYS USED TO LOVE CARROTS.

DUMPED!

I'M SO GLAD YOU'RE BACK, BUNNY. I PUT THESE POSTERS UP ALL OVER TOWN, BUT WHEN I SAW YOU IN THE WOODS...

LOST BUNNY

IF SEEN PLEASE CONTACT IS BRAMBLE CRESM...

...WELL, I KNEW YOU'D COME HOME.

I'LL GO AND GET YOU SOMETHING NICE TO EAT, YOU MUST BE STARVING BY NOW.

BUNNY

NAH, I BROUGHT SANDWICHES AND CHOCOLATE WITH ME...

HOME SWEET HOME

PSST! HEY, BUNNY!

I'VE COME TO BUST YOU OUT!

RANDOLPH!

AND I BROUGHT SOME FRIENDS!

WEENIE! PIG!

TWO AND A HALF YEARS EARLIER...

ABORT

...DIFFERENT.

DUHHH, WHAT'S IN HERE?

IT'S SKUNKY! GET DOWN!

DUHHH, WHAT DOES **THIS** BUTTON DO?

WHAT ABOUT THIS ONE?

GASP! HE GOT EVEN SMARTER!

BOOP! BOOP!

NO, PIG. HE SEEMS...STUPIDER.

WHAT DOES **THAT** SAY? DUHHH!

CLEVER-O-MATIC

AH WELL, IT'S SOMEWHERE TO SIT DOWN.

BZZZZZZ!

CLEVER-O-MATIC

DUHH...

RUMMMMMBLE!

IT'S OVERHEATING. IT'S GOING TO BLOW!

ATIC

WOULD ANYONE LIKE A BISCUIT?

NOT NOW, PIG.

ARGH!

EEP!

BONK!

CHOOM!!

I...AM... ...A GENIUS!!

SO, ALL THIS TIME, SKUNKY GOT HIS BRILLIANT BRAIN... FROM A MACHINE?!

HEY BUDDY! I SAW WHAT JUST HAPPENED. THESE ARE MY WOODS, I FOUND THEM. I DON'T WANT NO SKUNKS TEARING THEM UP.

'FOUND' THEM? I'M A VASTLY SUPERIOR INTELLECT NOW, I COULD RULE THESE WOODS.

YOU CAN TRY IT BUDDY, BUT I COME FROM THE CITY STREETS.

I KNOW HOW TO FIGHT.

OKAY, OKAY. LOOK, THERE'S NO REASON WHY WE CAN'T BOTH LIVE HERE, AS LONG AS YOU KEEP QUIET ABOUT WHAT YOU'VE SEEN TODAY.

AND WHAT DO I GET?

YOU GET THE GREATEST PRIZE OF ALL. TO INVENT YOURSELF! NO LONGER A COMMON STREET FOX, YOU CAN LIVE HERE AS WHATEVER CHARACTER YOU CHOOSE!

WELL, I'LL BE... THE GUARDIAN OF THE WOODS!

MYSTERIOUS! BROODY!

AND I'LL BE FRENCH, TOO.

CLASSY, Y'KNOW. LIKE ZIS.

EXCELLENT! LE FOX, YOU KEEP OUT OF MY WAY, I'LL KEEP YOUR STORY, AND TOGETHER THESE WOODS WILL BE OURS.

BON!

THERE IS JUST ONE THING.

ZAT!

I, UH... I GOT OUT OF MY GARDEN. I'M NOT SURE WHERE I AM.

HEE HEE! THAT BUNNY LOOKS LIKE YOU, BUNNY.

IT IS ME. TWO AND A HALF YEARS AGO!

LITTLE BUNNY, YOU DIDN'T SEE ME TRANSFORM FROM A STUPID IDIOT INTO A GENIUS DID YOU?

OR ME, ONCE A LOWLY FOX, NOW ZE GUARDIAN OF ZE WOODS!

UMM...NO? GOOD!

LET'S JUST MAKE SURE, WITH THIS MEMORY RAY I PICKED UP IN THE LAB!

NO!

ZZZAP!!

WH... WH... WHAT HAPPENED?

NOTHING. NOTHING AT ALL.

DAZED!

FORGET EVERYTHING.

EEE! VISITORS! I DON'T OFTEN GET VISITORS!

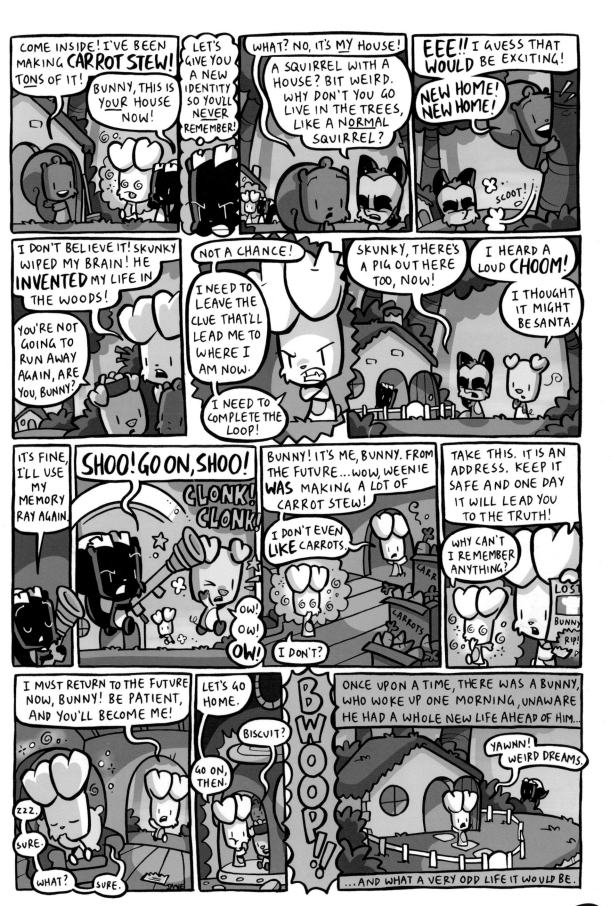

"SNOW MEANIES"

I BAKED MINCE PIES!

I'M DECORATING THE TREE.

I'M RUNNING AROUND IN CIRCLES!

BAH! HUMBUG!

SKUNKY, THEY'RE ALL GETTING REALLY EXCITED ABOUT CHRISTMAS.

AND IT'S REVOLTING.

HOW CAN WE RUIN IT FOR THEM?

WELL, WE COULD ALWAYS USE CHRISTMAS AGAINST THEM!

YOU HIDE INSIDE THIS BIG PRESENT, THEN WHEN THEY OPEN IT, JUMP OUT AND SCARE THEM!

MEH HEH HEH!

OOH LOOK, A PRESENT!

IS IT FOR US?

HEH HEH!

YOU CAN'T OPEN IT YET. CHRISTMAS DAY ISN'T FOR AGES!

AWW. OKAY.

ZZZZZ...

YET ANOTHER FAILED PLAN, SKUNKY. THEY DIDN'T EVEN COME CLOSE.

AND THEN I FELL ASLEEP.

IT WAS JUST A DECOY, TO KEEP YOU OUT OF MY WAY WHILE I INVENT..

WE ARE SUPPOSED TO BE FLYING OVER THE WOODS DROPPING A BAG FULL OF **WHIFFY EGGS** ON EVERYONE.

Y'KNOW, FOR CHRISTMAS.

EGGS TOYS

PONG!

BUT WE CAN'T EVEN GET T**HA**T RIGHT!

YOU DO BETTER, THEN. I'M SICK OF BEING YOUR DOGSBODY!

C'MON, LE FOX! WHY DON'T YOU FINALLY TELL EVERYONE THE TRUTH?

#!!

#!

☆⑤

NON!

HEY, WHAT'S GOING ON HERE?

ROAD BUILD THROUGH THE WOODS.

TONIGHT? BUT IT'S... ...IT'S **CHRISTMAS EVE!**

YOU CAN'T!

I'M THE RANGER OF THESE WOODS. YOU HAVE **NO** AUTHORITY HERE.

NO? I **DO** HAVE A BUNCH OF FIVES, THOUGH.

!!⚡💀!

#☆⑤!!

☆⑤!!

⑤💀!!

#☆!!

#!⚡☆

THIS ISN'T THE CHRISTMAS SPIRIT AT **ALL**. EVERYONE'S FIGHTING!

PRESENTS WOULD CHEER THEM UP!

!!
#⑤

WHAT DID SANTA BRING IN HIS SACK?

THESE TOYS ARE RUBBISH!

#💀!!
☆⑤!!

TOOLS

ARE YOU KIDDING? THESE TOYS ARE **BRILLIANT!**

SANTA BROUGHT ME ALL I ASKED FOR!

HUG!

YOU'RE SUPPOSED TO BE SANTA!

OH! OH, YES. HO HO HO! LET'S SEE WHAT PRESENTS I BROUGHT YOU THEN!

MEH HEH HEH! A FESTIVE **STINKY-EGG ASSAULT!**

A... **ACTION BEAVER?** WHAT ARE **YOU** DOING IN THERE?

EGGS TOYS

UH OH...

AN
EPILOGUE

"DOOR B"

WE FOUND A THING!

A **THING!**

ANOTHER THING?

PAF!

BUT WE ALREADY HAVE PLENTY OF THINGS.

NOT LIKE **THIS** THING! WE WERE EXPLORING THE OTHER SIDE OF THE WOODS AND WE FOUND...

...A BUILDING!

...A TEMPLE!

...A **BEMPLE!**

COME AND SEE, BUNNY!

DO I HAVE TO?

WE LEFT A TRAIL OF CROUTONS TO FIND OUR WAY BACK!

HM. I **DO** LIKE CROUTONS.

RIGHT! COINCIDENTALLY, AND COMPLETELY UNRELATED TO WHAT THEY'RE DOING, I'VE DECIDED TO GO. GOODBYE!

SKUNKY? WHERE ARE YOU GOING?

I'VE HAD IT WITH THESE WOODS, AND EVERYONE IN IT. I DESERVE FAR BETTER.

SKUNKY! STOP!

YOU WON'T KEEP ME HERE, MONKEY.

NO, IT'S JUST I WENT TOILET SOMEWHERE AROUND THERE.

BE CAREFUL WHERE YOU TREAD.

RRGH!

AND I AM **ESPECIALLY** SICK OF **MONKEY!** EVERYONE TREATS HIM LIKE THE DEVIL OF THESE WOODS, BUT LOOK AT HIM! HE'S AN IDIOT!

HOI!

HE HAS A POINT, MONKEY.

WHEREAS **I** AM THE GENIUS AMONGST US, AND I GET IGNORED!

WELL, NO MORE!

THEY ALL GO ON ABOUT BUNNY'S **HOME**. MEH MEH MEH! LIKE IT'S **SO** IMPORTANT BUNNY FINDS WHERE HE BELONGS.

PAH! WHAT ABOUT THE REST OF US?

↓ TO THE LAB

VMMMMM!!

WHERE ARE YOU GOING, SKUNKY?

THEY HAVE RUMBLED US, LE FOX. BUNNY KNOWS WHAT WE DID.

I SUGGEST YOU TREAD VERY CAREFULLY AROUND HIM.

I, MEANWHILE, AM GOING WHERE **I** BELONG.

AND I BELONG...

...BEHIND DOOR B.

SLAM!

(SEE EPISODE 44!)

MEANWHILE, ABOVE GROUND...

WHERE IS THIS THING, THEN?

MMM, CROUTONS.

WHAT THING?

MMM, CROUTONS.

CHOMP! CHOMP!

OH, HANG ON. IS THAT IT?

IS WHAT WHAT... **OHH! YES!**

IT'S ENORMOUS!

MMM, CROUTONS!

BZZT **LEAVE THIS PLACE!!**

SHRIEK!

SHRIEK!

SHRIEK!

RUN SCREAMING BACK TO YOUR WOODS! HIDE IN YOUR HOUSES! FOR YOUR YEARS OF COMFORT HAVE COME TO AN END!

FOR NEXT YEAR, YOU WILL BE **CRUSHED** **DESTROYED** AND **RULED**.

NEXT YEAR, YOU WILL **LIVE IN FEAR!**

NEXT YEAR...

...WILL BE **MY** YEAR!

—AND SO BEGINS YEAR 3: "THE **REIGN** OF **SKUNKY!**"

JOIN US NEXT TIME FOR THE MOST TERRIFYING SUPERVILLAIN -IN THE- WORLD...

DESTRUCTO

AND OTHER INCREDIBLE, AMAZING, RIDICULOUS STORIES.

BUNNY VS MONKEY ★★★ BOOK 5 ★★★ OUT SOON!

Discover more of Bunny and Monkey's hilarious escapades in...

Available now from the Phoenix Shop!

www.thephoenixcomic.co.uk